Four Favorite Fairy Tales

Retold by

Stephen Cosgrove

Illustrated by

Wendy Edelson

Goldilocks

Three Blind Mice

Humpity Dumpity

Billy Goats Gruff

IDEALS CHILDREN'S BOOKS
Nashville, Tennessee

Goldilocks and the Three Bears

Retold by
Stephen Cosgrove

Illustrated by
Wendy Edelson

IDEALS CHILDREN'S BOOKS
Nashville, Tennessee

Dedicated to my wife Shaerie, my Goldilocks.
Remember, always stay out of the bear's lair.

Stephen

Once upon a time, a long, long time ago, in a forest of pretty pines and poplars stood a cabin made of wood. Now in this cabin lived three bears: a big Poppa Bear, a medium-sized Momma Bear, and a teeny-tiny Baby Bear.

Late one day, after eating their supper of steaming stump stew, the bears prepared to eat their most favorite treat, peach porridge pie. But the porridge was too hot!

They sat around and blew on the bowls to cool them, but the porridge was still too hot. They decided to take a walk down the forest path and wait for the porridge pie to cool. They put on their coats, tied up their scarves, and waddled into the forest.

A time or two later, there happened on the path a beautiful, blond-haired little girl named Goldilocks. She spied the cabin in the woods and noticed that the door had been carelessly left open. She went to the door, looked inside, and shouted, "Yoo Hoo! Is there anybody home?" But, of course, the house made of wood was empty.

Against everything she had learned in school, Goldilocks walked into the cabin and looked about. There she spied three chairs set before a crackling blaze in the fireplace. There was a big chair, a medium-sized chair, and a teeny-tiny chair, and all were made of wicker and wood.

She sat in the big chair, but it was too hard! She sat in the medium-sized chair, but it was too soft! Then, she sat in the teeny-tiny chair, which fit her just right. So comfortable was she that she skrinkled and scrunched about in the chair until it broke with a crickle and a crack, and she fell giggling to the floor.

Goldilocks laughed and laughed as she dusted herself off and continued to snoop around the cabin in the woods. It was then that she spied the peach porridge pie cooling in the bowls on the table. She tasted the porridge in the big bowl, but it was too hot! She tasted the porridge in the medium-sized bowl, but it was too cold! Then, she tasted the porridge in the teeny-tiny bowl, and it was just right. So, she gobbled it up, gulpity gulp!

"Mmmm, that was good!" she said as she prowled about the cabin in the woods. She opened a door here and a door there, but all she found were closets filled with long woolen dresses, fuzzy fur coats, and pajamas all hung in a row. Finally she opened a well-worn door of hickory and shiny brass, and there she spied three beds, each covered with a patchwork quilt. There was a big bed, a medium-sized bed, and a teeny-tiny bed.

Goldilocks lay on the big bed, but it was too hard! She lay on the medium-sized bed, but it was too soft! Then she lay on the teeny-tiny bed, and it was just right. She scrunched her head into the goose-down pillow and fell fast asleep.

Goldilocks had slept for ten minutes, not a minute more, when the bears rumbled back into their house after their walk in the woods. They took off their coats and unwrapped their scarves and carefully hung them from pegs on the wall. Then they looked about the room and noticed that something was amiss!

"Hmmm!" said Poppa Bear in his big, gruff voice, "Somebody has been sitting in my chair!"

"Tsk! Tsk! Tsk!" said Momma Bear in a singsong voice. "Someone has been sitting in my chair!"

Then little Baby Bear looked with eyes opened wide and cried, "Someone has been sitting in my chair and they broke it all up!"

"Look!" growled Poppa Bear loudly. "Someone has been tasting my porridge!"

"Well, I'll be jiggered!" said Momma Bear as she rushed to the table. "Someone has been tasting my peach porridge, too!"

It was then that poor Baby Bear peeked his head over the edge of the table and cried out, "Someone has been tasting my peach porridge pie, and they ate it all up!" Unable to hold back any more, Baby Bear began to cry, and tears slipped and dripped down his fuzzy cheeks.

Poppa Bear waddled to the bedroom to get a kerchief to wipe the little bear's eyes. He stopped, looked once, and then looked again. "Someone has been sleeping in my bed!" he roared.

Momma and Baby Bear rushed into the room to see what the commotion was, when Momma Bear noticed her bed, too. "Fiddle dee dee!" she grumbled and rumbled. "Someone has been sleeping in my bed!"

It was then that Baby Bear, through tear-streaked eyes, spied his own bed. "Ah, ha!" said he. "Someone has been sleeping in my bed, and there she is!"

With a wink and a blink Goldilocks woke up. She leaped to the floor and skittered and scurried over and under the beds with the bears right behind. Out of the bedroom, under the table, over the chairs she ran for her life and escaped out the door never ever to return to the woods again.

There's a lesson to be learned
From this bit of folklore:
Don't enter strange houses,
And always lock your door.

About the Author

In 1973, Stephen Cosgrove stumbled into a bookstore to buy a fantasy book for his daughter but couldn't find one that he really liked. He decided he was looking for something that hadn't been written. "I went home and that night I wrote my first book."

Since that fledgling effort over a decade ago, Cosgrove's books have sold millions of copies worldwide.

Cosgrove was born in 1945. He attended Stephens College for Women in Columbia, Missouri ("A great year but I learned little and forgot a lot"), is married, and lives on a quiet little flower farm in Redding, California. There he writes on his computer, communicates by telefax with eight children's book illustrators about current projects, and takes healthy breaks to play with the dog and pick the daisies.

Titles In This Series
Billy Goats Gruff
Goldilocks
Humpity Dumpity
Three Blind Mice

Three Blind Mice

Retold by
Stephen Cosgrove

Illustrated by
Wendy Edelson

IDEALS CHILDREN'S BOOKS
Nashville, Tennessee

Dedicated to Robert, Michael, and René,
the original three blind mice.

Stephen

Once upon a time, there was a house, a pretty house, upon a hill. In this house there came to live a mouse and a mouse and a mouse. One, two, three. Can you see?

Now these mice that moved into this house were blind, so they couldn't see you or me.

To be pitied? No! For these were special mice, these three blind mice that wanted to live in this house.

One of the mice, simply spoken just a mouse, that moved into this house was named Alfred. Alfred played a harmonica all of his life. He could even play a flute called a fife. Alfred was one of the three blind mice.

Another mouse that moved into this house was called Missie. Missie could dance and glide like she was sliding on ice. She would spin and twirl not once, but twice. Missie was one of the three blind mice.

The last mouse that moved into this house was simply called Moe. Moe was as strong and fast as he could be. He could even run faster than a bumblebee. Even he was one of the three blind mice.

Now, the problem you see was that this house was really owned by a farmer's wife. She loved her house and she loved her life. What she didn't like was mice or any mouse in her house.

So, now the story of a farmer's wife and . . . three blind mice.

Three blind mice,
Three blind mice,
See how they run,
See how they run.
They all run after the farmer's wife, who drops
from her hand the butter knife. Have you ever
seen such a sight in your life . . . as three blind
mice?

Three blind mice,
Three blind mice,
See how they play,
See how they dance.
They tickle and giggle the farmer's wife. She
dances around to the sound of a fife. She has
never laughed so much in her life . . . as with
those three blind mice.

Three blind mice,
Three blind mice,
See how they laugh,
See how they sing.
They live a good life with the farmer's wife, who
plops jam on their bread with a butter knife,

Have you ever seen such a sight in your life . . .
as those three blind mice?

About the Author

In 1973, Stephen Cosgrove stumbled into a bookstore to buy a fantasy book for his daughter but couldn't find one that he really liked. He decided he was looking for something that hadn't been written. "I went home and that night I wrote my first book."

Since that fledgling effort over a decade ago, Cosgrove's books have sold millions of copies worldwide.

Cosgrove was born in 1945. He attended Stephens College for Women in Columbia, Missouri ("A great year but I learned little and forgot a lot"), is married, and lives on a quiet little flower farm in Redding, California. There he writes on his computer, communicates by telefax with eight children's book illustrators about current projects, and takes healthy breaks to play with the dog and pick the daisies.

Titles In This Series
Billy Goats Gruff
Goldilocks
Humpity Dumpity
Three Blind Mice

Humpity Dumpity

Retold by
Stephen Cosgrove

Illustrated by
Wendy Edelson

IDEALS CHILDREN'S BOOKS
Nashville, Tennessee

Dedicated to my mother. She has fallen from many a wall, but her shell has never cracked.

Stephen

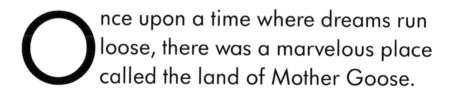

Once upon a time where dreams run loose, there was a marvelous place called the land of Mother Goose.

There was a king who was sort of funny. For this land was ruled by a fat little bunny.

In spite of his riches, this bunny king had but one friend with whom he could sing. An egg was his friend—all round and plumpity. The king simply called him Humpity Dumpity.

They wandered the walls, their feet plopping thumpity, and so goes the story of Humpity Dumpity.

Humpity Dumpity sat on a wall,

Humpity Dumpity had a great fall.

All the king's horses and all the king's men . . .

couldn't put Humpity together again.

The king was sad, or so it was said,
because he thought Humpity was dead.

But from the wall came flying on feathers and
luck a fluttery, feathery, web-footed duck.
Down he jumped and fell on his rumpity.
It was the king's dear friend—Humpity Dumpity.

So they ruled together in this land so funny,
Humpity Dumpity and the king—the bunny.

Billy Goats Gruff

Retold by
Stephen Cosgrove

Illustrated by
Wendy Edelson

IDEALS CHILDREN'S BOOKS
Nashville, Tennessee

Printed and bound in the United States of America.
Published by Ideals Publishing Corporation
Nelson Place at Elm Hill Pike
Nashville, Tennessee 37214
ISBN 0-8249-8271-1

Dedicated to my brother Mike, never a goat
because he always gets mine.

Stephen

Many, many years ago there was a land filled with mountains and meadows and a sparkling river that flowed right down the middle. On one side of the river there were waving fields of lush, green clover, and on the other side there lived the three Billy Goats Gruff with long, wooly coats and twisted taffy horns.

The only way to cross from one side to the other was on a rickety tickety bridge that was owned by a nasty old troll. The troll lived beneath the bridge in a musty, dusty hammock made from gray cobwebs and dirt, and he never let anyone cross unless they could pay a troll toll of a gold coin or something of real value.

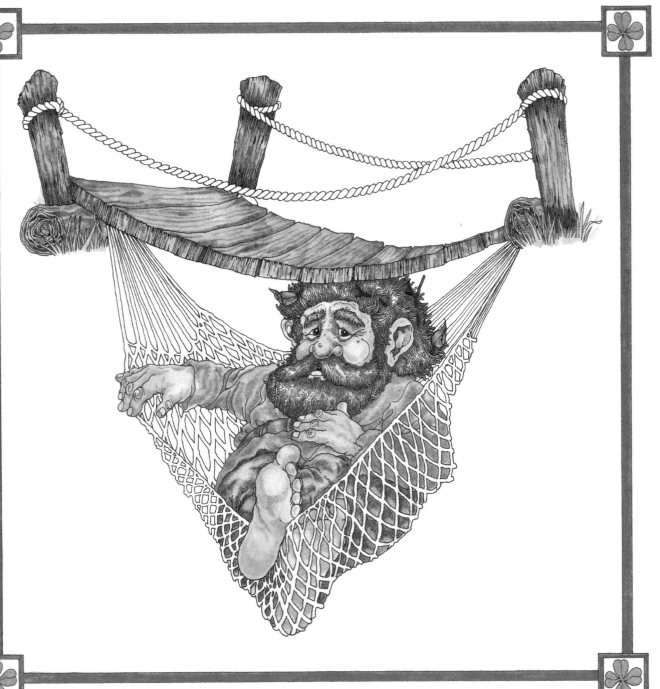

The three Billy Goats Gruff loved to romp and play in and around the boulders and rocks that lay scattered about their meadow. But what they loved to do more than anything else was to eat the sweet grasses that grew in great profusion on the hillside.

The biggest billy goat ate all the good clover and would butt the others out of the way. He got fatter and fatter.

The middle billy goat ate all the sweet, lush grasses that grew in clumps in the middle of the meadow and would butt the littlest billy goat out of the way. And he got fatter and fatter.

The little teeny-tiny billy goat only had weeds to eat and didn't grow much bigger at all. Sometimes he would just butt his head on the rocks in frustration. His horns got stronger, but he was very hungry.

The goats ate and they ate. They ate the flowers. They ate the grasses. Why, they even ate the roses that grew at the edge of the meadow. But there came a time when all the grasses were gone and there was nothing to eat on the billy goats' side of the river.

The billy goats' stomachs began to rumble and grumble because there wasn't any food to eat. They would stand and look with envy at the greener pastures that grew across the river on the other side of the bridge.

"If only we could eat some of that clover on the other side," the biggest, fattest billy goat said.

"If only we could eat some of the lush, green grasses on the other side," the middle-sized, plump billy goat said.

"Then why don't we just walk across the rickety old bridge to the other side?" the teeny-tiny billy goat innocently said.

"Because," the two fat billy goats chorused, "we can't pay that dumb old troll his toll since we don't have any gold coins."

"But," said the teeny-tiny Billy Goat Gruff, "the troll's toll is a gold coin *or* something of value. Surely, we have something of value?"

The two old goats looked at one another in a sly sort of way, for they had come up with a marvelous plan.

The fattest Billy Goat Gruff with his knees knocking together began to walk across the rickety tickety bridge: *Clickety click. Clickety click.*

A ragged voice bellowed out from beneath the bridge, "Who's that walking across my bridge?" And out popped the troll in a puff of dust. "Give me my gold coin or something of value or I'll be having goat stew for supper!"

"Well, I don't have a gold coin but I *think* I have something of value."

And with that the fat old goat gave that nasty troll the beautiful horns from his head. The troll accepted the horns in payment and then disappeared under the bridge as the biggest Billy Goat Gruff skipped across the bridge to the other side.

A minute or two later the middle-sized Billy Goat Gruff went right up to the bridge and with his knees knocking began to walk across the rickety tickety bridge: *Clickety click, Clickety click.*

The ragged screeching voice bellowed again, "Who's that walking across my bridge?" Then just like before, the troll pounced from beneath the bridge. "Give me my gold coin or something of value or I'll be having goat stew for supper!"

"Well, I don't have a gold coin but I *think* I have something of value."

And with that the plump old goat gave that nasty troll the beautiful horns from his head, too. The troll accepted the horns in payment and then disappeared under the bridge as the middle Billy Goat Gruff skipped across the bridge to the other side.

The littlest Billy Goat Gruff, with a hop and a skip, started to walk across the bridge: *Clickety click. Clickety click.*

From beneath the bridge came a screech and a holler. "Who's that walking across my bridge?" Like an ill wind that blew, he leaped upon the bridge. "Ah, it's the little Billy Goat Gruff, is it? Give me my gold coin or something of value or I'll be having goat stew for supper!"

"Well," said the littlest Billy Goat Gruff, "I don't have anything of value, so I'll just have to give you what my brothers gave you . . . my horns!"

With that he backed up a step, scratched his hooves a time or two, and then charged. He butted that dirty old troll right out of the story, and the only thing left was a puff of dust and a smudge on the bridge.

The three Billy Goats Gruff lived forever and a day on both sides of the river. Because the littlest billy goat hadn't given up his horns, not the biggest nor the middle goat ever again told him what he could or couldn't eat.

As you go through life
You'll pay many tolls.
At times you'll have to pay,
And at others you can butt the troll.

About the Author

In 1973, Stephen Cosgrove stumbled into a bookstore to buy a fantasy book for his daughter but couldn't find one that he really liked. He decided he was looking for something that hadn't been written. "I went home and that night I wrote my first book."

Since that fledgling effort over a decade ago, Cosgrove's books have sold millions of copies worldwide.

Cosgrove was born in 1945. He attended Stephens College for Women in Columbia, Missouri ("A great year but I learned little and forgot a lot"), is married, and lives on a quiet little flower farm in Redding, California. There he writes on his computer, communicates by telefax with eight children's book illustrators about current projects, and takes healthy breaks to play with the dog and pick the daisies.

Titles In This Series
Billy Goats Gruff
Goldilocks
Humpity Dumpity
Three Blind Mice